CHIRP!

Jamie A. Swenson

Scott Magoon

CHIPMUNK SINGS FOR A FRIEND

A PAULA WISEMAN BOOK
Simon & Schuster Books for Young Readers
New York London Toronto Sydney New Delhi

For my dear friends, thank you for joining my happy, sad, and bittersweet
songs—and for letting me sing along with yours too xoxo

Special thanks to Sean and Sylvie, who have been very fine friends to Chipmunk.

—J. A. S.

For Terri. Your song still inspires us.

—S. M.

SIMON & SCHUSTER BOOKS FOR YOUNG READERS
An imprint of Simon & Schuster Children's Publishing Division
1230 Avenue of the Americas, New York, New York 10020
Text © 2021 by Jamie A. Swenson • Illustrations © 2021 by Scott Magoon
Book design by Chloë Foglia © 2021 by Simon & Schuster, Inc.
All rights reserved, including the right of reproduction in whole or in part in any form.
SIMON & SCHUSTER BOOKS FOR YOUNG READERS and related marks are trademarks of Simon & Schuster, Inc.
For information about special discounts for bulk purchases, please contact Simon & Schuster Special Sales at 1-866-506-1949
or business@simonandschuster.com.
The Simon & Schuster Speakers Bureau can bring authors to your live event. For more information or to book an event,
contact the Simon & Schuster Speakers Bureau at 1-866-248-3049 or visit our website at www.simonspeakers.com.
The text for this book was set in Celeste. • The illustrations for this book were rendered digitally.
Manufactured in China
0421 SCP
First Edition
10 9 8 7 6 5 4 3 2 1
Library of Congress Cataloging-in-Publication Data
Names: Swenson, Jamie, author. | Magoon, Scott, illustrator.
Title: Chirp! : Chipmunk sings for a friend / written by Jamie A. Swenson ; illustrated by Scott Magoon.
Description: First edition. | New York : Simon & Schuster Books for Young Readers, [2021] | "A Paula Wiseman Book." | Audience: Ages 4-8. |
Audience: Grades 2-3. | Summary: A lonely chipmunk longs for a friend who will sing along with her.
Identifiers: LCCN 2020045644 (print) | LCCN 2020045645 (eBook) | ISBN 9781534470026 (hardcover) | ISBN 9781534470033 (eBook)
Subjects: CYAC: Friendship—Fiction. | Loneliness—Fiction. | Singing—Fiction. | Chipmunks—Fiction.
Classification: LCC PZ7.S9748835 Ch 2021 (print) | LCC PZ7.S9748835 (eBook) | DDC [E]—dc23
LC record available at https://lccn.loc.gov/2020045644
LC eBook record available at https://lccn.loc.gov/2020045645

Chipmunk lived on a rock.

Most days she sat on her rock,
chirping from dawn . . .

until the stars shone down.

Sometimes Chipmunk's songs were happy.

Sometimes her songs were bittersweet.

And sometimes her songs were very sad indeed.

The rock was a very good listener,
but Chipmunk longed for a friend
who would sing along with her.

One day Chipmunk said,
"Stay right here, Rock."

And off she went.

It wasn't long before Chipmunk came to a pinecone.
"Hello, Pinecone. Would you like to meet my friend, Rock?"

Pinecone agreed.

Chipmunk scooped Pinecone up and off they went.

Just as Chipmunk had suspected,
Pinecone and Rock
got on famously.

Chipmunk started to chirp, hoping that Pinecone would join her.

But Pinecone's talents, like Rock's,
were of the listening sort.

So Chipmunk chirped and chirped and chirped her own song.

It was bittersweet, for though she was happy that Pinecone and Rock were such good listeners, she still longed for a friend who would sing along with her.

"Stay right here," Chipmunk told Rock and Pinecone.

And off she went.

It wasn't long before she came to a log.

"Hello, Log. Would you like to meet
my friends, Rock and Pinecone?"

Log agreed. So Chipmunk tried to move Log. . . .

And tried . . .

and tried . . .

but Log wouldn't budge.

Finally Chipmunk sat and chirped
a song about loneliness and defeat.

A raccoon heard Chipmunk's song.

"That is a sad song," said Raccoon.
"It is the song in my heart," said Chipmunk.
"It is beautiful," said Raccoon. "Keep singing."

Chipmunk smiled and sang a bit more.
Raccoon swayed and tapped her paw.

When Chipmunk was done
with her song, Raccoon said,
"I will help you move Log."

So Raccoon and Chipmunk tried to move Log. . . .

And tried . . .

and tried . . .

and TRIED . . . but Log simply wouldn't budge.

Chipmunk and Raccoon sat. Chipmunk started singing
a bittersweet song about friendship and defeat.
Raccoon listened for a moment, and then joined in harmony.
She added a bit about frustration.

A moose heard their song.

"That is a very sad song," said Moose.
"It's the song in our hearts," said Chipmunk.
"I added the part about frustration," said Raccoon.
"It is a beautiful song," said Moose. "Please keep singing."

When their song was done, Moose nodded thoughtfully.
"Maybe I can help move Log," he said.

So Chipmunk, Raccoon, and Moose tried to move Log. . . .

And tried . . .

and tried . . .

until

POP!

Log rolled down a hill,

across a meadow,

and stopped right next to Rock and Pinecone.

Just as Chipmunk had suspected, Rock,
Pinecone, and Log got on famously.
"They are perfect together,"
said Raccoon.

"Like a rock, a pinecone, and
a log in a pod," said Moose.

Each day Chipmunk still chirps her songs.
And Rock, Pinecone, and Log listen.

Sometimes her songs are happy.

Sometimes her songs
are bittersweet.

And sometimes
her songs
are very
sad
indeed.

But now Raccoon and Moose sing along too.